EREV

The Evening Years of Reuben Gurewitz

Anne Shmelzer

RAILWAY CREEK BOOKS CANADA

RAILWAYCREEKBOOKS.CA

This edition published in 2021 by Railway Creek Books Canada
2191 Quinn Crescent, Ottawa, Ontario, CANADA K1H 6J5
RAILWAYCREEKBOOKS.CA

Print ISBN: 978-0-9947601-4-2
Ebook ISBN: 978-0-9947601-5-9

Print and digital editions designed and produced by
Allen Zuk • ALLENZUK.COM

CONTENTS

CHAPTER ONE 8

CHAPTER TWO 15

CHAPTER THREE...22

CHAPTER FOUR 35

CHAPTER FIVE..45

CHAPTER SIX...50

CHAPTER SEVEN 56

CHAPTER EIGHT...59

CHAPTER NINE..65

CHAPTER TEN...71

EPILOGUE 75

GLOSSARY 77

ACKNOWLEDGMENTS 80

AUTHOR BIOGRAPHY 81

For my mother, Ena Frances Cook,
of blessed memory

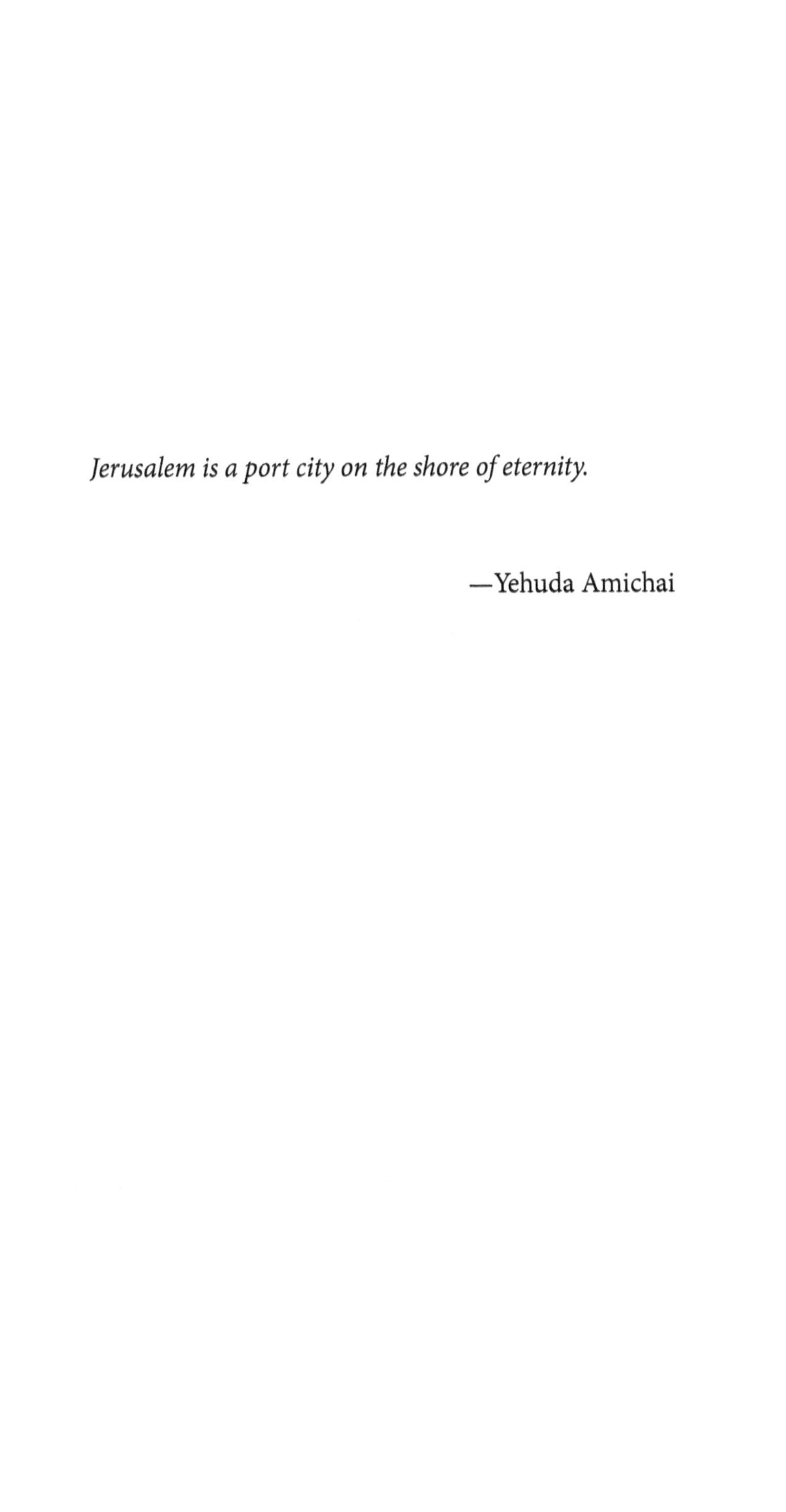

Jerusalem is a port city on the shore of eternity.

—Yehuda Amichai

1

When the eighty-three-year old physician, Reuben Gurewitz, awoke that August morning of 2016, he knew full well there had been no change in the conditions that oppressed the citizenry of metropolitan Ottawa. Outside the window of his ground-level bedroom, just as the weatherman had predicted, the sky was cloudless with no possibility of rain. *Just more searing temperatures, Reuben. It's been nothing but heat waves since early May. And Reuben, these constant winds…*

So, here was Ruthie again, eh, speaking to him from the grave. Was he still grief-stricken for her even after these five long years? How was it possible that he could still hear her husky voice so distinctly? And with the entire eastern North American continent plunged into a horrific, formidable drought, the likes of which had not occurred since the last century, he wondered how he would cope.

Reuben shifted position, intent on stretching each muscle of his body against a firm mattress which he should never have bought. *Nothing but aches and pains since.* Slowly, he went on to perform his morning exercises on that uncomfortable thing, gritting his teeth to withstand the pain in his ankles and knees…and everywhere else. *At the very least,* he thought, *I am alive within the stillness of my ground-level bedroom.* He thought of Ruthie more so at this early hour when he would turn his gaze to the open window which provided a view of her rear courtyard garden, exactly as she had planned it. This morning, the perfume from the decaying wisteria blossoms on the vine against the house wafted through the open window.

That old wisteria had wound its way into the eaves. That thing would pull the shingles off the roof, trail over the rain-conductors, rip into the gutters; its roots would eventually heave the cobbles right off the surface of his courtyard. Just as sure as hell. He should force himself to get rid of it. But how could he? Ruthie had planted it.

In his mind's eye, he pictured the wisteria he and Ruthie had once seen while driving through the old-world South on one of those car trips they used to take when they had still been young. When their bodies had twisted in ecstasy. Had it been *that* long ago, the Eighties, when they had decided to take the backroads across Georgia? They had come across an old, deserted house, and there in a field next to the buildings sprawled a wisteria vine so tangled that its rampant, unrestrained growth had covered more than an acre. Ruthie spoke for years of that impenetrable, jungle-like wisteria, so he'd best not forget to get the arborist in to cut that damn wisteria up there on his own wall this autumn, or he'd be sorry—he surely would.

Yes, he was very much concerned about his property these days, especially since Ruthie had enhanced the rear courtyard with gardens between the house and the new garage workshop she had had built for him. Behind the garage, the lush, hundred-year-old maple drooped its branches over the back lane. She had taken so much pleasure from the back lane, the snarl of lilacs against pin cherries, the chokecherries, black currants and such like that lined its descent all the way to the street. He truly loved that old back lane. He must get himself out there this evening, surely just to walk the lane again.

Kingdom *plantae* popped into mind, startling him to find that his Latin still hovered around in a memory he feared was fast fading. Though, in truth, he must accept that his memory was betraying him. Inevitable. Perhaps, instead of this penchant for self-criticism, he should think of himself as a medical man of moral action and make some meagre attempt toward the survival of *this* world. Reuben pictured his beer-drinking neighbour across the rear lane who waves from his upper-duplex porch these hot summer nights. Usually, that fellow points his finger to Reuben's uncut grass along the laneway, but Reuben now believes in the value of every single blade of grass.

Photosynthesis. Reuben pieced together its meaning from scant knowledge. Chlorophyll, within chloroplasts of plant and leaf cells, absorbs light energy from the sun and is responsible for giving plants their green colour. Chloroplasts serve somewhat as collection centres within a plant cell, store energy, act upon water in roots by splitting hydrogen from oxygen inside a water molecule. Carbon dioxide, exhaled by animals and humans, is absorbed into the leaves of plants and with hydrogen produces sugars. Food for plants. The leftover oxygen is released into the atmosphere for the survival of the world. *How innocently unselfish,* Ruthie had murmured. He remembers most every word from Ruthie. So if that *drunken neighbour man* points his finger to Reuben's uncut grass, that's a *good* thing for the environment.

Reuben rolled over on his hard mattress and spoke his *modeh ani,* the prelude to the morning prayers. From the age of three, his father had taught him to recite this prayer, and as he had grown older, his father had taught him the complete morning and evening service which they had recited together. Reuben remembered his mother being in the room. *Tweed* cologne, he had read on the bottle when his mother twisted the top off and sprayed her wrists. He sensed her nearness even now.

Fully awake, Reuben felt his heart within his chest—a long moment of nothing, then a flutter between beats—and he pictured the old, hollowed-out muscle, hoping it would prove loyal. One must be cautious at such an age. As a physician he knew not to provoke himself with extraneous concerns, especially those which he had no control over. He inhaled slowly, deeply.

Take the closure of the old *shul.* The decision had been settled abruptly by a cavalier board of directors. He missed the leisurely walk to *Shabbos* services as well as to the weekday prayer services each morning and evening, and a kibbitz with the guys over breakfast. The loss hit him hard. It just didn't seem right, driving on *Shabbos* in direct contradiction of *halachah!* Thumbing a nose at Jewish Law at this point of his life? Having to take the car out and drive away across town on that dangerous Queensway to the West End synagogue where the prayers were different? Never in his wildest dreams had he figured on driving, on having to drive on *Shabbos.* Reuben stood up slowly, faced east and whispered, *s'lichah* to seek forgiveness for driving. He began to recite *Shacharit.*

* * *

Finishing morning prayer, fatigued, he sat down in the easy chair beside the window. He knew that he should be going upstairs to the kitchen to get his breakfast. He must not permit the intrusion of mood swings. After all, a medical education had trained him to be circumspect, of paramount importance for the benefit of his patients, and also for his own well-being.

A case in point: Early on in his medical practice, a family had consulted him after the sudden death of their thirty-six-year-old brother. *Fred got up early as usual, ran downstairs, reached for the newspaper at the front door and keeled over.* The challenge presented by these young men, worried about their own genetics, forced a wary approach to the case and had been exhaustive, to say the least. Thus Reuben strained to discover and to impose an exact *hippocras* for treatment: heart regulators, daily regimes for walking, exercise, an olive oil enriched Mediterranean diet, meditation, prayer, and lastly, *don't forget the benefits of pleasure, gentlemen. Remember, laughter has proven to be the best medicine.*

When sunlight reflected off the venetian blinds, Reuben shifted position in his easy chair, leaning forward, pounding his feet against the floorboards before rising and making his way to the window, the one that Ruthie had always left open for the night. And his first apparition was of their wedding anniversary trip to Jerusalem. He had planned meticulously. He had purchased airline tickets on an El Al flight out of Toronto's Lester B Pearson International Airport, and reserved a suite in the guest house at *Mishkenot Sha'ananim*, facing the walls of the Old City. What a memorable trip that had been.

Out the window, Reuben noticed that the wisteria had entangled the pergola. Choked, neglected. Reuben turned away and shuffled across the room, stumbling across the threshold on his way to the spa. His new L.L.Bean moccasin slippers, an eighty-third birthday gift from Jonathan in Los Angeles, were too large. Reuben entered the spa, washed his face, his eyes. As he splashed over the sink, he visualized Ruthie sipping frothed milk from the rim of her Booths "Real Old Willow" coffee cup she'd bought at Birks. She had sat in her Stickley rocking chair, feet resting on the matching stool, from which she most certainly would have remarked upon the sale of Henry Birks and Company to a foreign buyer. Reuben remembered her precise placement of the cup and saucer on its silver tray.

He heard her soft, measured words: *Look out the window, Reuben. I pray for the roses. Even the rue has dried up. Dust with every passing car. There is not enough water to clean the streets anymore. Remember the Eighties when one truck would come down the street to brush and vacuum, and another followed behind with water? Nowadays, the gutters are filled with packed dirt. The medians are weed infested. What in the world is going on, Reuben?*

Reuben studied his lined and wrinkled face in the mirror. His image reminded him of Jonathan, who recently had been urging him to make reservations for the two of them to travel to Israel. Reuben leaned in closer to the mirror as he drew the razor between nose and lip.

A brown layer of pollution had settled over Ottawa that autumn. Ruthie had begun to speak of visiting her former kibbutz in Israel, but she didn't seem to want to return for a visit when Reuben had offered to make arrangements for the trip, and he had had to find other means to ease her mind. He remembered that on one particular hot and windy day he had proposed a drive south to visit Smyth's Apple Orchard near Morrisburg. Ruthie had been anxious to see whether the winds that season had damaged the crop.

They had found the pomologist in his shed bent over a bin of apples from which he sorted out the ones with scabs. "These southerlies will be my ruination." He spoke with inaudible fury, moved slowly as he pitched his profits for that year into a nearby rusted trailer. "Worldwide climate change is here to stay, and how am I supposed to deal with that?" he had muttered.

Reuben remembered the drive back to Ottawa that day through a landscape of parched fields, low water levels in lakes and rivers, especially noticeable as they crossed the bridge over the Rideau River at Kemptville. Ruthie beside him murmured,

It may sound meshuga but, in my humble opinion, evidence of climate change began about 1964, after the assassination of John Kennedy. I noticed the lack of rain back then, and a few years later after Martin Luther King—a chochem if there ever was one—and a few months later, Bobby is pistolled at arm's length.

Nearing the city, Reuben pushed the car northward through the suburbs, and he didn't let up as he turned eastward along the Queensway. *Don't be so tense, Reuben. You are driving too aggressively.* He braked hard under the carport. He felt her hand tighten on his thigh when Ruthie said, *I think we should visit Israel as soon as we can, say next April?*

* * *

Reuben reached for the worn Royal Velvet towel and dried his face. He ran hot water over his straight razor, set it across the shaving cup. *But he is walking behind the hearse,* moving in slow motion so slowly he pushes forward with all his might until he stands over her and sees her as slowness permits him to see her in life, her lustrous head of hair with reddish streaks among black, unable to abate his agony as he hears a shovelful of soil thump, a shovelful thumps, thumps, thumps, thumps. Beside him, Jonathan, heartbroken, grips the shovel in his hand.

Jonathan, mein sohn, sleep beside me for the seven days of shiva.

Instead of Israel in April, Jonathan had brought him to his home in Los Angeles.

2

"That's it," Reuben spat out to his reflection. He left the spa and walked to his computer in the adjacent room. He booted up and Googled Sirhan Sirhan, smoldering gun in hand. *I did it for my country.* Strange: Reuben hadn't remembered Sirhan Sirhan screaming at the television camera. Reuben read on: *California State Prison, Corcoran. The infamous inmates have included Charlie Manson, Juan Viego Corona, who murdered twenty-five people in 1971, and Sirhan Sirhan.*

During the early Sixties, Reuben had spent three years in an internal medicine residency program at a Los Angeles hospital. This was the era that saw the rise of social justice through decisions of the Supreme Court under Chief Justice Earl Warren. These were the years of the presidency of John F. Kennedy, who in his inaugural address had coined the motto *Ask not what your country can do for you, ask what you can do for your country.* Even though this ethic promoted fairness and the public good, Reuben came to realize that he was living in a county that encouraged mercantilism and was fast becoming a society driven by acquisition, greed and open corruption.

They stood by and watched as the shopping centre became a place for Jewish kids to "hang out" on the Sabbath. He and Ruthie had been driven mad by traffic jams. When a black colleague came to visit and the building manager told them,

"No more coloured visitors in this building, or you're out," it sealed their determination to get back home to Canada as soon as possible. The clincher that still made his stomach heave had occurred during his emergency work on the night shift when a male senior staff member had cozied up to a young Mexican woman. When she rejected his advances he had cursed her with invective Reuben had never heard in his life even to this day.

After years of medical school, internship and residencies, Reuben became a specialist in internal medicine, eventually returning to Ottawa with Ruthie and their newborn son, Jonathan. He became a Fellow of the Royal College of Physicians.

A community Hebrew school in Ottawa provided their treasured son an education in English, French, and Hebrew. Reuben remembered eight-year-old Jonathan, mechanically inclined, figuring out the espresso machine—not too many drank this type of coffee back then. He and Ruthie hosted dinner parties and discussed current affairs with their friends, and Jonathan was always under the table or silently sliding onto Reuben's lap.

Jonathan now lived and worked in an unrecognizable America. What if that Donald Trump won? Would he really build that fence on the Mexican border? What would happen to the illegals who live and work the fields? Would they detain them, send them back? In this turmoil, what would become of the children? Reuben swallowed, reminded of his own family in Bukovina and the children who had been ripped from the arms of their mothers. *Even in Suceava,* his mother had told him. *That's the reason we left—and were we ever lucky.*

On his way to the kitchenette, the slipper fell off. Stupid, to rush around. Reuben turned back to his computer and emailed Jonathan. *It's about the slippers, mein sohn. Remember? L.L.Bean, Jonathan, a half size too large. Order another pair, please. See you in two weeks. Love, Pops, and don't forget the Remy Martin, it's half the cost down there.*

At the kitchenette counter again, Reuben fumbled with the power button on the espresso machine. There he went again, losing his concentration, this time wondering whether Jonathan might consider taking a trip to Israel this coming winter. It would be Spring there. Carefully, Reuben removed the milk from the bar fridge and filled the stainless-steel pitcher. When the red signal light went out indicating that the water was hot, he heard, *Ten to seven, Reuben.*

Ruthie raised the window blind and said, *It's minus ten Celsius, Reuben. Snow mixed with ice pellets.* She adjusted the fireplace thermostat and turned to the radio. *Damn!* She punched the OFF button. *Bye-bye CBC. We shouldn't have to listen to such stuff so early in the morning. And Reuben, even Tom Allen in the afternoon is changing? Can't he just play the music without his incessant chatter? Why only one movement? Why not play the complete symphony? Yesterday, I couldn't believe he only played the Rondo from Mozart's Horn concerto. Once again, Reuben, Tom played it again.* She sighed, sipped the coffee. *Delicious, Reuben, thank you, darling.*

Ruthie had loved the aroma of fresh coffee beans, the smell that lingers throughout these lower-level rooms of the house: the office, the sleeping room, the spa, especially pungent in the kitchenette where he now found himself grinding the beans into the portafilter. He had not altered much in the rooms from the original placement Ruthie had decided on; the books were ordered on the shelves, her jewelry arranged in the black leather box, exactly as she had left them. Reuben had discarded her clothing, all but her carefully-folded scarves, a few favourite sweaters. He thought of the spa where her towels were still tightly rolled on the ledge of the whirlpool; her toiletries, the bottle of *Uremol* lotion, even her last bar of olive oil soap—the one he had bought in Loblaws—was tucked into the old wicker basket there.

Reuben carefully inserted the portafilter into the espresso machine. He smiled as the dark, foaming coffee dripped into his preheated cup. He then pressed the steam switch and waited for steam to build up. Holding the pitcher of cold milk under the nozzle, he opened the steam valve, rotating the pitcher slowly, then up and down, until a thick foam developed. He poured the frothy, creamy milk liberally, sweetening with grated chocolate upon which he spooned a favourite pattern. He then carried the tray to the sleeping room and set it down on the game table. He sipped from the cup.

Reuben stared out into his courtyard garden. *Not enough rain, hardly any.* He recited the prayer for this necessity. He said his *modeh ani*. His practice had been always to lay *tefillin*, but his physician had suggested that at his age, he eat breakfast first. Before the old downtown *shul* had shut its doors, he had always walked to prayers. Now, with the closest synagogue halfway across town, it didn't seem right. A man should be able to walk to his morning and evening prayers, but how could he make a move to another home at his age?

He pondered over his day. Should he bake a whole wheat? Strange, a man alone making bread, still keeping kosher. Ruthie had kept the meat dishes separated from the milk, nagged him to follow her routine, placing utensils, pots and pans, and such items into their designated cupboards and drawers—*fleishik* and *milchig,* a separate set for *pareve.* He probably made errors, *nu*? But if a man upholds as best he can the laws of *kashrut,* should not the Holy One who rules the universe give a nod in his direction? Sometimes?

Reuben left the sleeping room to wash the coffee items in the kitchenette before leaving to climb a flight of stairs to the main floor, a slow climb for him these days. Was there wisdom in his decision not to move into a retirement facility, as Jonathan liked to suggest every time he had an opportunity? He reached the head of the stairs, sweating, and made his way through various rooms to the rear of the house.

Out the kitchen window, miniature apples gleamed among the branches. How and why had the sun turned so hot this summer of 2016, even hotter than the searing heat of previous years? And where were the birds? He toasted a bagel, spread it with lots of butter, a spoonful from a jar of his new batch of orange marmalade. What else? Orange juice, vitamins, prescription pills. He meant to review these many bottles and packets at his next appointment with Dr. Ellis. He would try to convince Dr. Ellis of his strength and virility. Why not? Hadn't his father remarried at the age of eighty-three? He hoped to meet a gentle woman who would share his interest in art and literature—not a *yente,* and definitely not a *kvetch* like he tended to be, not a shirker. He reminded himself of the application for the mathematics course, long overdue now, the missed Hebrew program at the Jewish Community Centre last year after the High Holidays. Mental activity lends purpose, steadies the mind.

Ruthie's apple pie? He wondered if he could prepare one. He must drive to Smyth's once again. He had telephoned and spoken with the grower who told him that he was still "hanging in," even adding more heritage apples and pears to his orchard. Ruthie had loved the old varieties: McIntosh, Northern Spy, Talmond Sweet, Snow. *Choose for flavor, crunch and texture. It's simple, Reuben, with a well-floured board and the recipe. An egg and vinegar mixed with ice water, a bit at a time into your bowl of flour and shortening until the pastry forms a ball. Careful!*

Culinary skill? What did he know about cooking and baking? He had neither her organizational skills nor precision. It was all he could manage to play his violin these days—later, maybe Bach, but he felt tired. Awake at two-thirty again. Strange. He usually only suffered from insomnia during the winter solstice, the season of the Maccabees, but striving to manage the Christmas hustle and bustle, and heavy traffic on slippery roads. Hard for an old man.

Reuben had lain awake, mulling over the horrific radio newscasts he had heard recently. Now called *stories* by the press, short clips were speedily delivered, peppered with clichés and jargon. Each and every day, Reuben vowed not to break a lifetime habit, and so he listened as atrocious events were brought forward which, quite frankly, demeaned and trivialized, including recently the airing of sexual antics of pre-teenagers. Qualitative selection seemed to no longer apply. All news was Fit to Print: suicide bombing; air strikes; the Russians are at it over Syria again; the Isis boys burn hospitals and post as they behead men, women and children. Christians are chased to a mountain top where they linger for months with little food or shelter, and not even the Pope intervenes. What was one to do? Speechless, Reuben held his head in his hands.

Reuben turned off the bloody news. *Shameful!*

Reuben pushed away from the breakfast table for now he caught himself thinking of the well-off professionals eating at Rib Fests—*a full rack for $20.00.* He must not allow his mind to falter. How should he spend the remainder of this day? What would Ruthie have suggested? Call Sophie, meet at the Pantry for a bowl of mushroom barley, a quiet *schmooze.* Sophie would criticize his *kvetching* about conditions on the street, the poor, the hungry, the homeless, the addicted, and she would discourage him from worrying over refugees from Africa on boats that were sinking, bodies floating in the Mediterranean. The lucky ones were coming into the Italian ports of Lampedusa and Pozzallo. What the hell was going on?

Would there be war? Reuben shivered because he now saw in front of his face Ruthie's rueful expression.

Play me Beethoven this evening, Reuben, Ruthie would call as she padded up to the top floor to practice yoga. His mind was jumping to thoughts of her again. He must clear away the breakfast dishes but he didn't move. He saw the blank, brick wall of the house next door, the white ceiling of his own back porch. Not anymore, the street didn't hold much for him, the neighbourhood, the park, the river, and the river path. Not since the day the dog had jumped and mauled Ruthie.

For reasons which he cannot understand, this is the time of day that he recalls the policeman at the door. If only they had buried the dog under the frozen bank of the Rideau River. Stupidly, Reuben took up his empty plate and studied the pink design—Ruthie's favourite. He saw her standing on the snow-covered riverbank, and she is waving from the far side of the Minto Bridge where he no longer walks.

3

*S*chool's *just around the corner, guys. Comin' fast. Summer's gone, and I sure hope yer kids are ready. Mine done good last year, and boy oh boy I hope they do good again—*

Reuben snapped the OFF button of the radio. It seemed to Reuben that each and every morning he was greeted with a string of trite comments. Words and phrases were oftentimes mispronounced and grammatically incorrect. Surely in this year of 2016, announcers could strive to abide by linguistic rules and deliver their content with clarity and precision. Or would media slang sink our language further into a state of vulgarity?

Reuben remembered CBC radio as it had been in the Fifties and Sixties when personalities such as Lorne Greene, who, upon returning from war service, resumed his radio career. There was also Max Ferguson hosting *Rawhide*. Canuck seniors from coast to coast surely must remember the forty-odd years of *Gilmour's Albums* hosted by Clyde Gilmour. Reuben thought then of Bruno Gerussi, an entertainer and actor who had uplifted the radio audience from blues and boredom over nineteen years until his retirement in 1971. Beloved Peter Gzowski on *Morningside* three hours a day for fifteen years had been a definitive *Voice of Canada*. Reuben could only conclude that after living a long life with these illustrious broadcasters, listeners were belittled.

Reuben reached for his daily journal. Thumbing pages, he hesitated at one of his entries from this past June after a massive sinkhole in front of the Rideau Centre shopping complex had closed Rideau Street:

The pavement has collapsed and forced evacuation of the area. To top it off, a van, fortunately driverless, has fallen into the sinkhole. Subsequent dangers include a gas leak, power outage and a water main break. Work on the tunnel for the new Light Rail Transit system has to be suspended until the cause of the sinkhole has been determined and repairs completed.

Infrastructure projects have tried the patience of citizens as they find themselves facing street closures, ever changing traffic diversions, massive congestion, a shocking number of accidents and casualties, some being fatal. *Rampant disorder everywhere*, thought Reuben, flipping the pages of his journal.

Findings from a recent study released last month by the American Medical Association reveal that prayer cannot be proven to be of benefit to those suffering from heart disease.

Reuben pictured himself walking the ward with his medical staff man as they conducted early morning rounds at the National Jewish Hospital, Denver. They entered the room of an asthmatic patient to find him standing beside his bed, unwinding the leather straps of his phylacteries. After the examination and outside in the ward corridor, Dr. Ritkin had said, "A little of this kind of faith, Gurewitz, increases the potency of digitalis. Never underestimate the power of faith, young man," he added quietly.

Reuben got up from his chair, shuffled to the back door. "Bingo! *Mishegaz* about prayer from the AMA," and winced, finding himself sounding dotty. Outside, he looked up to the sky where contrails from jetliners patterned an east-west trajectory. *How many are flying back and forth across the Atlantic today? Another issue, this pollution.* He reentered the house, crossed the room to where his prized Bose radio rested on the music cabinet, selected Claudio Arrau's *Final Sessions*, and slid it into the player. From now on, every day, he would listen to a disc from his classical collection.

Reuben settled onto the couch and rested his old legs on the ottoman. *Turn off the radio, shut down the TV, the computer, trash the newspaper*: He would follow this plan for one week from this coming *Shabbos* to the next. He'd eat what he could find; he was getting too stout or, as Jonathan purported, *portly*. That package of chicken breasts had been in the freezer since April. Reuben shivered, feeling strangely cold, but in this heat? He felt too tired to fetch his sweater.

Jittery, his heart beating rapidly, he closed his eyes against the sudden glare of sunlight through the Venetian blinds, but he was too late. Waves of white light signaled the beginning of an ocular migraine. He waited for the lines to dissipate, as would the kidney-shaped light and the piercing pain that would follow. He waited to allow his body to release its tension. He listened, but could not hear the roar of traffic descending onto King Edward Avenue from the Mackenzie King Bridge, only high-pitched tinnitus. This too would go away after a half-hour or so.

He awakened to scratching on the windowpane. American Goldfinch, a flock in the branches of the columnar apple, nipped at the brown, rotting fruit. The tiny birds flickered brilliant yellow, like those from years ago at their Sainte-Agathe chalet, the sanctuary that they had had to abandon in the winter of 1993 when fire had burned it beyond repair.

* * *

Nearing the Mirabel ramp of the Laurentian Autoroute halfway to Sainte-Agathe-des-Monts, pellets of ice began to slice across the car windshield. Did the traffic slow down? Did drivers reduce their pressure on the accelerator? Not a one. Speeding vehicles pass Reuben to the right, to the left. It's as if *les Péquistes*—bigoted to say it, but as if an army of Separatists could sense his political persuasion. They have spotted him through the iced windshield as a diehard Federalist—a curse on that Bouchard for his foment yet again.

A van passed on the left at a wicked clip. What could that driver see in this whiteout? A few shadows, a pair of pink globular headlights behind at fifteen to twenty feet. Idiots.

"Reuben, get off at the next exit. Stop, already. This is dangerous. I'll have a breakdown."

"Ruthie, *shah,* he's doing the best he can," says Sis from the back seat. "It's nerve-wracking enough without you bawling."

Why had he agreed to start out so late in the day? Nothing would do but they must go up north. *For a few days, Reuben, for snow on the fir trees, to hear the whine of the wind. The ice will be freezing on the lake. Humming, cracking, crunching, and loud bangs as the lake freezes into the depths of green-black water.* He'd make a roaring fire in the hearth, open a bottle of vintage. Sis would spend an hour preparing her fruit salad, a sponge, and Ruthie would lay the blue antique dining table with her Limoges from the sideboard. Drowsy by the fire, warmed, he'd play a new cassette: Claudio Arrau's *Final Sessions,* playing Schubert's *Impromptu, D.935.* Sis would fall asleep in the leather chair.

Safe arrival. The driveway had been snowplowed by faithful Gaetán. Ice crystals on the leafless beech tree glimmered against the headlights. As Reuben got out of the car, he noticed that his neighbour's garage door was gaping wide open. Empty.

The three of them lugged in the groceries, Sis's valise. Gaetán had laid kindling in the fireplace. Out the window, large snowflakes danced ring games, blotting out the lake below where the diving board towers over the water. Reuben set the kettle to boil. He walked across the living room and lit the fire. From the bedroom, the scrape of drawers being pulled open in the butternut dresser. Ruthie sings *Mi Y'Mallel*. Chanukah is coming.

Reuben had just placed the teapot of Darjeeling on the tray, a packet of Walker's shortbread, when Sis opened the back door and threw a valise across the kitchen floor to where he was standing.

"There's smoke coming out of the roof next door, Reuben. It's shooting out of there. Call the fire department. Call the operator. Oh Reuben, call 911."

But he ran out the door, climbed the steps to grab a look for himself. Sis is right. The neighbour's place is afire.

They stand in the driveway, all three, dressed in their coats and scarves and hats and boots and mittens. Flames devour the neighbour's house. The north wind is fierce now.

"When are they coming, Reuben? Call the police."

Not a sign of a car, not a sound of a motor. Silence.

"We stand and watch their property burn, Reuben," cries out Sis.

Where the hell are they? By his watch, that makes forty minutes since he'd called the fire station.

"Call *la Sûreté*, Reuben. I'll take the car. I'll go to the corner to get help," said Ruthie.

The cold, he saw, had frosted her nose. He took his mitten to rub her face. He blew his hot breath over her. "Ruthie, Ruthie," but he heard a crash. The neighbour's roof crumbles. The side of their own chalet catches fire. Aflame.

A firetruck arrives, but it was not a tanker truck—no water and no fire extinguishers. *Le camion de pompage ne marche plus;* the pumper truck won't start. *Trop froid;* too cold. The volunteer firemen must carry hoses and generator down a steep incline to the lake and pump water up one-hundred and fifty feet.

A police car pulled alongside. "Qu'est ce qu'arrive; what's happening, monsieur?" shouted the officer.

Many villagers arrived throughout the night. They came in their trucks and cars. They carried whatever they could from the smoking house, even the piano. They worked into the morning despite freezing temperatures, Reuben toiling alongside, never stopping until everything possible had been removed, everything except the contents of their upstairs bedroom where he and Ruthie had slept, bathed, loved—in those days, mad love, when his body had been supple, muscular, and he had known his Ruthie, the touch of lips to chest, a clear, liquid recollection of Ruthie over him, his eyebrows kissed, his eyes caressed by her tongue. *Reuben, my friend, my everlasting life, I love your cells, your vessels, my breath, my soul...*

* * *

Out the window, the wisteria shriveled away in the eleven-o'clock, furnace-like heat. Sis had always struggled into the courtyard to view the wisteria, coming each Friday evening for *Shabbos* dinners. He should order a couple of rib-steaks from Loblaws Kosher, but who could he call to join him?

Sis had remained faithful after Ruthie passed away—the sixteenth of February, 2011. Sis had helped cook and clean up even though it would always be a late evening because he attended *Maariv* and the services would end after sundown, very late in summer. Did he ever enjoy walking back and forth. Now, there was no *shul*. His old Lower Town synagogue had closed a couple of years ago and amalgamated with the conservative *shul* way over in the West End. What was a *yiddisher* to do but to keep on driving across town to pray. Dangerous in the dark. Sadness. *Tragerkeit umet!*

Reuben and Ruthie had been grateful when Sis finally moved from Montreal to come and live near their home on Stanley Street in New Edinburgh. The residence overlooked the Rideau River and stood within sight of Government House, with Parliament outlined on the western horizon.

Sis had given him comfort, but she too had died last year.

* * *

After his evening meal that day, Reuben had set out to take his usual stroll, but once outside, he stopped at the sidewalk to inspect the frontage of his property upon which he had expended so much effort and money since its establishment years ago. Seaside Bar Harbour Juniper, planted above the two-foot stone wall, had provided a dense, cascading coverage and resistance against excessive amounts of street salt spread by the road gang every sub-zero winter.

Reuben then turned into his front garden pathway that lead to the maturing ginkgo under which there had been planted *geranium sanguineum*, now a profusion of stunning purple-red blooms. The hops vine, planted to provide privacy for the screen porch and, in former years usually burgeoning, now drooped in thin, wiry disarray. This year the vine would need rich fertilization and pruning in the autumn, as would the wisteria in the rear courtyard. He made a mental note to call Artistic Landscaping, a company which rewarded fidelity with fine services and expertise in horticultural selection. Reuben felt grateful for their trouble-free, in-ground watering system which still functioned effectively as well as a glistening cotoneaster hedge they had planted along the north boundary of the property, a choice that tolerated the cold, north winds of an Ottawa winter.

He proceeded northward through the pathways of New Edinburgh into the exclusive residential area of Rockcliffe Village where he would stroll for the better part of an hour before turning eastward through Manor Park and back home. It seemed the sky was already darkening. Were the days already becoming shorter? He checked the time of his watch. He still wore an old-fashioned Bulova—much to Jonathan's disapproval—but he had again forgotten to wind it. Another slip-up.

An all-day rain is best for the crops and vegetables, Reuben. Recently, he had begun to hear his mother's voice. He missed her gentle constancy, and her presence. She had been the first to alert him about the fungal Dutch elm disease that was decimating the forests throughout southern Ontario in the Eighties. She had warned him of oncoming weather extremes and made him aware of the melting of the polar ice cap.

Reuben asked himself how one could deny climate change when faced with worldwide drought, wild fires, and closer to home, ten-minute deluges with gale-force winds. Even at night heavy winds occurred, a three-day heat wave in the month of May with record-breaking temperatures, and last winter with little or no snow coverage high winds swept away exposed topsoil off farmland and caused forest fires that destroyed large land masses, sometimes coming exceedingly close to a city. Calgary, Alberta for instance. Floods, hurricanes, landslides. What next? Will the next president in the White House acknowledge consensus from the scientific world that we are presently undergoing a rapid, evolutionary, global change, or ... not at all? And is the next president of the United States of America to be Trump, who, according to the radio announcer, *is sure getting a bunch of attention* as a first-class repudiator. The sky darkened. Was summer already coming to an early close?

Reuben was following his usual route north through Lindenlea, and as usual was careful to place each foot firmly for fear of falling. It was hard to keep track of changes, like the recent alteration in the seasonal change from standard time to daylight saving time, which had been switched from the end of April to the middle of March. Gosh, he worried about the kids having to stand and wait for their school bus in black dark.

Societal shifts discombobulate people. There had been the new national flag, a crimson maple leaf on stark white; a switch from imperial weights and measures to that of metric; introduction of the loonie one-dollar coin in place of that lovely paper dollar with the portrait of our Queen.

It seemed to Reuben that a kind of secular humanism had replaced the religious institutional practices that stood since Confederation. Who *is* marrying today? Who receives a burial service? Not too many. Does anyone care if a child is born out of wedlock? The maple is now an endangered species. There was the closure of Canada's major newspapers: *The Ottawa Journal* and *Winnipeg Tribune* in 1980, *The Toronto Telegram* in 1971.

A foot is a foot and three make…sort of a metre, as the imperial system of weights and measures is pushed further into the recesses of memory. *A pocketful of loonies and a man gets rid of them fast.*

Reuben's medical patients had complained bitterly about their children's chaotic classrooms and the absence in the curriculum of reading, writing and arithmetic. Once on a visit to Jonathan's high school, Reuben had found the guidance counsellor sprawled out on a couch in the main office speaking with the vice-principal, who had his stocking feet up on his desk. Uproarious. A neighbour child had once jumped up on Ruthie's kitchen counter and proceeded along from one end to the other while his mother continued to sip from her cup of tea.

In the late Eighties, Reuben once caught a hospital staff member in the act of forging a prescription on one of his pre-printed pads. He could only think of the decline of communitarianism alongside that of the institution of family along with a loss of long-established manners. All in pursuit of individualism.

Reuben stopped and stared at the neat, pleasant houses along the street, one painted with red trim, a black door. This curative walk allowed an old body with worthless, grumpy thoughts to beat the blues. After all he was in pretty good health, with blood levels being checked by his young physician.

Reuben resolved to take action by nightfall. He must address his torpid behaviour, his stubborn and obsessive thought patterns that jumped from one subject to another. Frankly put, this all added up to a depression with the classic symptoms: lack of interest, vague fatigue, insomnia, loss of appetite related to missed meals that were improperly chosen and prepared with haste. He resolved to return to the Centre, schmooze with the old gang over lunch at Hillel Lodge and then go swimming in that magnificent Olympic pool, maybe take a few lessons. He could eat at the Israeli style café where the food was delicious and nutritious, and afterwards visit one of the best Jewish libraries in Canada, right there and all under one roof, not to forget the lecture series, the adult education classes.

He did not want to turn into a first-class *schlemiel* by his continuous reiteration of past events, the losses, the deaths, none of which could have been prevented, avoided, or changed. Jonathan had made a career move and his wife had agreed. Jonathan had been offered a career in documentary filmmaking that no one should ever turn down, a genre that Jonathan understood, having previous experience and superb talent. Jonathan had risen to become a talented director. So it happens that he's in Los Angeles on the far side of the continent. Not easy for an old dad, but Jonathan had been gone fifteen years, and he had not only a beautiful wife, Ellen, but three sweet children, *kineh hora,* so he's not coming back, not by a long shot, not even if Mr. Donald Trump became the next President of the United States of America.

Jonathan, his quiet, steady son, even in infancy taking his milk and sleeping, more milk, sleep, take more, sleep. Later on, he played, play alone, play with kids, follow everyone and every moving object with his beautiful almond-shaped eyes. Build with blocks, electric wires, build a playhouse. *I don't like to talk much, Dad. Am I normal?* On his first day at high school, the fifth formers in grade thirteen thought he was so adorable they had placed him on their wide shoulders and carried him around to the classes and the schoolyard. *Dad, I think I'm a hit. I like that place, Dad.* He had a sparkle in his eyes, pep and spring to his walk, and a great group of friends who had remained friends to this day, each and every person, nearing fifty years. Reuben had a ticket for his next trip booked for October, and Reuben loved Jonathan's home in old Hollywood, the grandkids and his wife, Ellen.

Ruthie had suffered the loss of Jonathan. She had tried hard to stay active and cheerful, but it was not the same the vivacious Ruthie, tossing her head with a witty comment. Reuben blamed himself, his own negligence for not seeing the danger in that off-leash dog park. Shock, weakness, loss of blood, and then what the hell kind of infection had she suffered? He was stunned when the autopsy revealed rampant staphylococcus. From a dog.

Most definitely a mad dog that was allowed to go off leash, but, he had not wanted to lay a charge. He hadn't wanted to drag himself through a court case, nor did he want to inflict Jonathan. "Better to say Kaddish, son, and allow her to settle in *Sheol*, ascend with the words of your prayers of praise to our Sovereign, full of compassion."

"Yes, Dad, I'll go to prayers every morning and night. You don't have to fear. I love you, Dad," he had said on the night he had taken the flight home.

"We are both official mourners, Jonathan. This is our way. It is both of us who say *Kaddish*. You are her blood and soul. Understand. That is why you have the obligation, Son."

Jonathan replied, kissing him and holding him.

Reuben had fallen asleep, comforted, and slept soundly throughout that night.

* * *

Reuben continued his walk through the now moonlit streets of his neighbourhood, passing the gated walls of Government House that followed its perimeter along the street which led south to Stanley Street and his home. He paused to breath in the sweetened scent from the potted jasmine plant he had set at the back entrance. An excellent walk and he felt duly tired, he thought, eyeing the green wingback leather chair as he passed into the family room. He poured his ounce of Remy and sat down.

Out of the blue, Belleville sprung to mind. He ought to revisit his old home as he had not been there since June of 2005 for the celebration of the fiftieth anniversary of the Sons of Jacob synagogue on Victoria Road. Eleven years was a long period but to him time was fast fleeting even though he did not live in the fast lane like some of his acquaintances seemed to prefer.

Surely someone he had known would still be in Belleville. He had been told that membership had dropped to a mere thirty families. He would leave tomorrow and see for himself and he would stay a few days to try to make contacts. He just might be able to find someone who had known him.

4

At five-thirty Wednesday morning, Reuben eased his 1968 MGB GT out from under the carport. He had decided to take the back road to Perth instead of tackling the heavy volume of speeding traffic on the Queensway, Ottawa's east-west expressway that linked with Ontario Highway 7 traversing the Province.

This Queensway, developed in the Fifties and Sixties, was also a major artery of the Trans-Canada Highway leading upriver to North Bay, Sudbury and Sault Ste. Marie and westward to Victoria, British Columbia—the longest highway in the world, costing over a billion dollars and completed in 1970.

This was still in the time when drivers thought of themselves as responsible. They had been schooled to understand that to save one life is to save an entire world. Not so many years ago, an accident causing death or severe injuries on a Canadian highway had been rare.

The engine purred as he accelerated onto Vanier Parkway, thanks to the team of mechanics at Redshaw's for the attention they lavished on his precious automobile. He guessed they were proud to work on this old beauty.

Reuben ran into congestion even at this early hour, and soon traffic slowed to intermittent standstills for the better part of half an hour. The entire area was undergoing considerable infrastructural changes. He inched forward into one lane before the construction site for the rapid transit corridor linking Riverside Drive to the grounds of the General Campus of the Ottawa Hospital, an artery requiring construction of both road overpass and railway underpass.

Another huge project affecting the area was the laying out of an east-west light rail electric train system. Consequently, at Hurdman Station, goodbye pristine parkland because, when all is said, only a narrow green strip would be left for recreational use along this section of the Rideau River. Reuben felt that what was touted as progress would result in additional ecological losses, perhaps a negative impact on some heritage sites.

Finally freed from traffic congestion, Reuben travelled the miles—he still calculated in miles, not in kilometres—turning west and crossing the Rideau River over the Hunt Club Bridge. He turned south onto Prince of Wales Drive, west on Fallowfield Road, all the while carefully changing lanes as he drove through the monotonous uniformity of sprawling suburbs to cross the bridge over the north-south Veterans Memorial Highway 416, continuing along Fallowfield and turning south into the countryside along the Old Richmond Road. Whew! The inbound road was choked with commuter traffic and so many school buses.

School buses? Jonathan had walked back and forth to grade school, indeed coming home for lunch. Entering Lisgar Collegiate high school, Jonathan either rode the city bus alone or biked back and forth. No one had given thought to personal danger in those days: A pervert would find another pervert and carry out some type of perversion together without bothering anyone.

He stopped at a restaurant in the market town of Perth. Great coffee at this establishment, Michael's, and he spent the better part of an hour savouring an omelette prepared with fresh vegetables, a side plate of fresh fruit. Truly satisfied, Reuben strolled the main street to view restored stonework buildings—masonry being an historic craft of the original Scottish settlers, many of whom had been veterans of the War of 1812 and had settled in Perth after the dissolution of their regiments. Reuben walked further on and found a bookstore owned by Leslie Wallack. Browsing the shelves, he picked up a copy of *A Marginally Noted Man* by one Anne Shmelzer, an Ottawa author. The book came highly recommended. *Well done, Anne Shmelzer.*

Having resettled in his car, he left the Town of Perth and followed the signs to Highway 7. Here was the highway for citizens traversing southern Ontario, connecting Ottawa to Peterborough and continuing westward across the top of metropolitan Toronto through towns and over the hills and dales of the countryside to end at Sarnia on the shores of Lake Huron, a non-stop drive of over six hours.

Within the hour, Reuben noted that the farms and fenced agricultural fields soon yielded to a rugged landscape of cliff and rock amidst dense deciduous and coniferous forest. He passed McGregor and Silver Lakes, dismayed to see the shorelines of both lakes now built up with side-by-side permanent dwellings, few of which remained the original cottages of past years. In the following hour, Reuben drove through an isolated area with few services. Years ago, he had avoided hitting a cougar that had jumped off a granite outcrop from fifty feet above and moseyed across the highway in front of him to disappear into muskeg. *Did cougars still roam the area?*

Needing a break, Reuben pulled into the roadside park at the Salmon River just west of Arden turnoff. He walked over to the shoreline and gazed into the trickle of clear water dripping over exposed rocks. His first impulse was to say the prayer for rain. He then returned to the car to get his camera and took photographs of the dry riverbed which he would submit to the *Globe and Mail,* not just to the local papers.

His father had told him stories about this Algonquin tribal region whose people had sold furs to him. Recently, Reuben had read that the Obaadjiwan First Nation, a non-status community, had declined a Reserve designation in 1844. He wished he'd paid more attention to Dad, asked more questions. His father had told him that in the early days he had travelled far north over rough trail and through dense bush. How had he got the furs back out, being so far away from Belleville? *Who remembers?* his father would have muttered. His father preferred to forget.

Circumstances had improved in the aftermath of the Second World War as profits from the tailoring business enabled his father to buy a new 1949 Ford Meteor. Reuben had just turned sixteen that October. Boy, had he been proud when Dad had put him in the driver's seat. Driving north from Belleville Dad had said, *Keep your mind and senses alert, Son.* Not so easy when all the way to Madoc his father had expounded on driving tips, Mosaic law on conducting commercial undertakings from *D'varim,* instruction on male comportment before the age of eighteen, disadvantages of early marriage, marrying out of the faith, et cetera. *Keep your mind active. A means is through history. The twenty-four books of the Tanach is a history book. These are your people and this is your locality, Hastings County.*

All the while they had headed westerly, Dad kept on recounting the highway's construction. *This Madoc to Perth section began around 1931, put a few dollars into pockets during the Great Depression, the pockets of over twenty-seven thousand men, Reuben. Back-breaking and dangerous at every turn, the undertaking proved successful. The crews managed most of the work by hand, blasting through rock, dredging muskeg, swatting blood-sucking insects. They worked fast and finished at Perth by August of 1932. Of course, you know the road was built along the existing right-of-way of the Canadian Pacific Railway. Most people doubted they could succeed putting a road through all these swamplands and rocks. The formidable Shield, Reuben, it's called…*

Reuben remembered that he and his father had stopped to talk with a homesteader who was building a barn much like the one back over there by the Salmon River. Today the river had hardly any water in it. But Reuben remembered that his father wound down the window as the fellow placed his foot onto the running board and said, *This is Shield country, sir, and I'm lucky to find a finger of fertile land. Come on in for a spot of tea.*

Dad had consented but kept swiping his brow and smiling all the while as they sat in the homesteader's once-abandoned cabin, lonely and broken by neglect for their cup of tea with that hopeful man and woman with their five kids scampering around. Who could expect a yield from the thin layer of topsoil that would barely feed a family through a long, harsh winter.

Now, in these present times, it would only be scavengers coming through a bent gate to strip the house for the barnboard to decorate their urban walls.

Reuben drove leisurely along, enjoying the remaining miles through this preferred route before turning southward through Tweed and toward Belleville, leaving this section of The Land Between, bioregion with its exclusively significant ecological features in the greater complex ecotone that falls within east to west boundaries between the Ottawa Valley and Georgian Bay, and from north through the *Canadian Shield* southward to Lake Ontario. He pulled to the shoulder and left the car to examine thirty-foot high exposed bedrock of varying shades of grey and pinks.

* * *

Reuben pulled the car sharply to the shoulder of the road above the shoreline of the Moira River. The once rippling river now lay barren on her desert bed. Reuben inched closer to the guard rail. Forlorn-looking kids rode bicycles and popped wheelies on the dry river bottom, having the time of their lives. Reuben suddenly felt chilled, despite the pervasive heat.

When Reuben registered at the Ramada, he was told that a severe water restriction had been imposed. The City of Belleville, the desk clerk told him, was now in a Stage 3 drought, pointing out the window to magnificent Lake Ontario in an agricultural heartland where, predictably, bountiful crops grew due to a temperate climate, rich soil mixes of clay and loam, and plenty of water running southward off the Shield down the streams and rivers and into the Lake. These recent years, with more frequent occurrences of lack of rain combined with huge hot air masses, a significant result of urbanization, Reuben feared the long-term effect. Could people return to washing clothes in one tub of water? Could they go back to one bath a week? How about that dishwasher? How about that air conditioner?

In the hotel room, Reuben lay down. *A parade:* In his mind's eye, he saw his father carrying a Torah scroll through the Belleville streets led by a brass band. Cheering, applause, laughter, sugar-spun candy on a stick, and then, a dimly lit room, his father wrapping him in his *tallis* and saying the evening prayer.

Reuben had been raised in privilege by his father, a tall, straight lion of a man, known in the Region as a just person, a fair trader, kind and generous to his employees. To Reuben, his father had guided him with tough rules administered fairly and with tenderness, always. Actions counted, never words. Although his father had not much adhered to ritual, he had lived by the Mosaic law and had taught Reuben by his own example. Hopefully, Jonathan would follow in those footsteps.

In the few hours before dinner, Reuben drove over to the main business street to find Russell's Electronic Shop whose owner belonged to Sons of Jacob, the synagogue where Reuben's family had been members. The congregation had only twenty-five members now, the shopkeeper said sadly. Thanks to an anonymous donor, and generous at that, the small community still owned the building. They still brought in a rabbi for the High Holy Days. They conducted a few Friday night dinner services throughout the year. The hope was to bring in new members as the city seemed economically vibrant, but it would take effort and ingenuity to rebuild a functional community like the one Reuben had experienced as a young man. He discovered that many had moved to Toronto since 2005 when Reuben had last visited the community. The older folk have followed their children.

"The shul is kept locked now," the kindly shopkeeper said, "except for the High Holy Days and special occasions." Reuben handed him his business card and Russell promised to mail the notices of any upcoming events. Reuben felt a twinge go through his *kishkes,* for the shopkeeper spoke with the same quiet voice as Jonathan. Reuben longed for his son, and he sorely missed his father and their old way of life in Belleville.

Years ago, Reuben had pledged to peddle his father's menswear line so that his father and mother would not be burdened by his university fees and expenses. Reuben relished independence and responsibility. He remembered his father saying, *You manage affairs, Reuben, and you start young.* His father had taken out the back seat of the *Meteor* so that there would be enough room for the goods.

Reuben had spent the first year after Senior Matriculation—that would have been the summer of 1951—learning everything about the mechanics of an automobile so that if he ever had a breakdown, he would know what was wrong and how to fix it. *How not to be duped when you're out there on the road and the country boys take you for a city slicker.*

That was how he had met Laura Burns during the summer of 1956 when Reuben pulled in to her father's store in Eldorado. Burns General Merchandise and Grocer. She had told him that she studied Latin on her own time. Laura had disclosed decisive plans for her future education.

"I intend to become a teacher, but I shall be educated. Not like the ones I put up with around here. How do you pronounce *Gurewitz*, please, Reuben?" She then asked him the origin of his name.

"I was named after Uncle Reuben, my dad's brother, who was killed in Rumania."

"How in the world was he killed? Why?" Laura interrupted.

"Because he was a Jew. Dad saved the newspaper articles from the American press that reported the killing rampage by a mob of four thousand strong that day in Suceava. June 11, 1930." Reuben studied the puzzled look in Laura's eyes.

"Dad wanted me to know why he had taken action to leave the land in which his people had lived for centuries. From my earliest memories, my father told me the truth about the vitriolic hatred that had caused him to bring me and my mother to Canada where people don't hate as much. Back there, it led to the genocide of the Jews of Europe."

"I never heard that before. Oh, dear friend, how horrible."

"It doesn't make the headlines, I'm afraid, Laura." He realized that Laura knew nothing of the fate of his people. He turned aside to hide his dismay that Laura, as a citizen of Canada in the year of 1956, knew absolutely nothing about the Holocaust.

"Please, don't be sad, Reuben Gurewitz. You must tell me about that time. You must stay on for supper and stay overnight for it's getting too late to move on up the road—isn't that so, Father?" Laura motioned for Reuben to come inside the store.

Standing in the doorway, Mr. Burns nodded. He did like the lad, but meant to make the best price and needed time to examine and place the order properly.

Later, across the supper table, Laura asked Reuben for the derivation of his surname. She certainly was an intelligent person, he thought.

"I understand Gurewitz is somewhat synonymic with Horowitz, and it seems that Jews who wandered into a Bohemian town known as Horovice would have taken this designation. The town existed as early as the twelfth century under Count somebody or other. I can't remember his name. This manner of naming became common for Jews. For example, *Reuven of Horovice* would have been a way to be designated in early European culture. Of course, a Jew would have a Hebrew name. Mine is *Reuven ben Yosef*. I'm Jewish and proud of it. Hey, do you go to camp, Laura? I went to Camp Hagshama on Otty Lake near Perth."

"Well, my friend, no one should ever have his own name taken from him, I'm sure." She tossed her pageboy hairdo.

* * *

Boy, had she been cute, Reuben thought to himself, realizing he was tired and hungry at the end of this unusual day. He wondered where Laura Burns now lived. He fumbled for the telephone book on the hotel bedside table and leafed the pages of the Madoc section. He found an L. Burns listed there. He wrote this number in his book.

5

Laura had taken her chair and placed it in the shade on the eastern side of the house where she could at least feel a slight breeze once in a while. *This extreme heat takes the breath away*, she thought, the thermometer registering between thirty-five to thirty-eight degrees Celsius. The same weather condition had blanketed this part of the country all this August of 2016. Now the month was coming to an end and perhaps a change might be in the offing, she hoped.

Parched fields worried her. How would Russell survive this coming winter? *Only three-quarters of an inch of rain all summer*, he had said, when he had finished cutting the meager crop last week on both his own land and hers. The soybeans had shriveled. No cash crop this year. She might advance him a bit of money to carry him through, poor fellow, trying to make a living in drought conditions. She admired Russell as he had shown bravery to take on her fallow fields and try to reap something from them. Laura was grateful that he had tried. It was the least she could do for him, her neighbour, who lived directly across the road and who in each of these past thirty years had planted her fields and kept her barn in shape.

She gazed at the barn that had served this property since 1864. Her grandmother had told her that Ebenezer Dedham had lugged the stones from off the surface of his fields to lay the foundation. The old stoneboat was still in the barn.

Laura wondered at this feat, not to mention the barn beams Ebenezer and his neighbours had erected, one of which measured sixty feet long and two by two feet thick. Hoist and tackle were still there.

The barn nestled into the slope of the hill above a thicket of lilac that overgrew the foundation of Ebenezer's first house. The barn towered over the property, perhaps imposing itself over the acreage, imprinting a message—a metaphor surely for protecting and preserving this place. But to protect and preserve this place begged cash. And this responsibility was her constant worry. Day-in, day-out, a struggle that frankly given today's climate extremes, not to mention acid rain, if and when you did get any rain, seemed futile. She hoped it wouldn't suck the life out of her.

A branch of the black locust swayed slightly. She smiled and sniffed. She caught herself sniffing often these days, sniffing to be resolute, determined to maintain a position of stewardship of this land. After all, this property had been settled since 1830 when Ebenezer Dedham had received the Crown Grant. She sniffed again. She caught herself—it aggravated her to no end that the original parchment had somehow fallen into the hands of a local collector who would not, even under her threat of suit, release it. He just would not hand it over. Period!

Laura looked at the long laneway that sloped upward to the Hastings Road. Her way out? No, never. She would turn seventy-six next month. She had lived alone and she had stayed alone all of her born days, and so be it.

The lane leading from the barn to her fields would soon take her to the swimming hole. That would be a welcome dip. The maples along the lane, she noticed, had already begun to turn—but what? Brown, an orange brown? Lack of rain, or was it years of acid rain that had distressed the maple trees.

Tomorrow she just might take the car and make a tour to see what the devil was actually going on.

Laura must see that she had enough gas. The Rav4 was in excellent condition and had just been serviced at Belleville Toyota. Bruce looked after it, a dependable mechanic who had worked there for years.

She was proud of the driveshed and kept the hundred-year-old building in repair. Anderson had put on a new steel roof last year. Like the new roof on the house, she had chosen a dark antique green. She had forgotten the designer name for the colour because it really didn't mean very much to her. How confusing and amusing those designer names are.

She stared at the driveshed where she parked the Rav4. Inside a second set of doors stood the buggy that her father had given her for her horse which she still used on the odd occasion, still keeping Old Maggy, a good horse, in the barn and having Russell tether it outside to pasture and visiting Old Maggy early mornings, each and every day, the poor thing. There were far too many items in that driveshed, but it was too late. What could she do but sell them, and it was too much trouble, never fetch a price: old harness, yokes, milk cans, equipment from the distant past. Someone, one day, would reap the benefit.

She got to her feet and picked her cane off the hook on the wall behind her. A walk to the swimming hole? She felt steady enough, not dizzy as usual, thanks be.

The lane to the swimming hole descended past the driveshed, past the attached outhouse toilet, now unused, which the old people had visited, and which had been kept sanitized with wood ash and Gillet's Lye far down into the deep hole in the ground.

At the halfway point down the hill, challenged by the heightened heat and humidity, she considered returning to the house, but she breathed in deeply and set her foot down firmly.

Her confidence improved with the nearness of the river but after reaching it, standing over it, from the bank and overlooking it, the river confronted her by its evidence of drought. She turned her back on the river, her own Moira, and vomited, and when she stopped retching, turned to look once again.

The river was down by half or more, and the banks had dried out. She could detect, perhaps, a slight current but it seemed still water, swampland water, polluted water. She must not allow anyone into the property to swim this season. In her lifetime, she had never seen the big rock on the far side fully exposed. Now the rock sat on the dry riverbed, a flat mass of eight feet in diameter from which all the kids had dived and frolicked. This proved that the authorities were correct in addressing the current weather conditions as a Stage 3 Historic Drought.

Laura leaned heavily onto her cane for the scene triggered dizziness, shortness of breath, pressure in her chest. Never had she felt the sun so intense.

She sat herself down under the beech tree at the bank and viewed the murky water, smelled its fetid stink. Another wave of nausea hit her, and she thought that perhaps, soon, she would travel away. Against her will, she would leave here—her house of fifty-three years. The foul water, diseased, tempted her. She began to weep over the water as though the river had been a personal friend and she had found that friend dead, the dead body of a beloved, and it truly did seem to reveal a hidden past when Reuben had written that he was going away. She winced. This thought proved that she was not losing memory, not if she still conjured visions of a faraway Reuben.

The dream had returned earlier this morning at dawn. Her mother slept beside her in the bed. *Mother, I have to call the hospital to see if he is still alive. Is he, Mother? Is Reuben still alive? I must reach him.* Laura had awakened and wept.

Even at this early hour, the sun, blazing through the window, blinded her. She had forgotten to lower the window shade. *If I ever see the sun at dawn again rising to burn and bake the land and the very soil under my feet to set the world afire…* She quieted herself, lest blasphemy escape from her mouth. She made a mental note to read William Faulkner's *As I Lay Dying* once again.

Every afternoon during summer holidays, her mother would hitch the horse to the cart, and her mother would drive her here to swim. Laura had adored her mother. *You are my true woman of valour, Mother*, Laura whispered. In later years, Laura had ridden the horse the two miles up the road from their store in Eldorado, walked it steadily down the hill, dismounted, ran along the bank and dived into the river—every afternoon, rain or shine, and mad as hell when Sundays had prevented her from doing so.

6

Abruptly, Laura turned away from the river and began to walk across the first field toward the broken-down fence. She picked her way across the cedar rails. A farm gate was another project that she had not been able to complete. So many repairs and projects.

Making her way up the grade, she noticed a car parked with nose facing her and it was four o'clock in the afternoon. Who could it be? Laura resisted the urge to hurry because she winded easily, especially climbing this hill. A man leaned on the hood and watched her, waving. A minute or so passed, and she saw him slowly making his way toward her and mouthing words, but she couldn't hear what he was saying.

They met, and really the terrain was too steep here, so it took a few moments for them to gain a foothold and face each other.

"Laura, I rang your phone but there was no answer, and so I took the liberty of driving in. I hope that's ok."

What was a body to do when greeted like this on a steep hill, with a beating heart, shortness of breath, vision blurred, some deafness?

"If you are indeed Reuben Gurewitz, please understand," she cried out. "It's a steep hill, my heart beats, I can't hear or see well… Let us walk up together safely."

They were drenched with sweat and huffing and puffing by the time they reached the yard. She took Reuben's arm and led him to the stairs and onto the porch where they both collapsed into chairs.

"I apologize, Laura. I'm impulsive as an old man. My judgement's off, truly."

"I'm going to fetch us a glass of water, Reuben, as soon as I catch my breath. I've just had a shock. Not only you. I just went down to check the river and the river has almost dried up on me." She hunched forward, elbow on knee and leaned her head against her hand.

"It's all over the countryside, Laura," Reuben whispered. She sat back and studied him. He appeared sad.

"I'll get the water, Reuben," but he followed her softly into the kitchen. He stayed beside her as she opened the refrigerator door, as she opened the cupboard door and removed glasses, as she poured, as she handed him the water.

Reuben took her free arm and led her to the table, took her glass from her hand and set it down. He held the chair for her to sit beside him. She sipped from the glass.

"It's fifty-seven years since you left, Reuben."

"March 5, 1959," he whispered, not looking up.

"I'd saved my salary from three years of teaching in Coe Hill, living with Mom and Dad."

"I don't know where to begin," he replied.

"Let's not even try to," she said and laughed. "Why did you come, though, now, to see me?"

"I've been thinking, Laura. Memories seem to be my obsession these days, and you are at the centre."

"Remembering seems to be our work at this stage of our life, Reuben, it seems, to my mind, anyway."

"Well, you are obviously not inactive, Laura. I stopped at the Madoc Township Hall and the secretary told me you are running the farm here. Tell me, who is at your old store? Why have they let the place run down? Who is the lady? She told me she didn't even know you."

"Rural life in these days is nothing but a string of houses, Reuben. No one any longer knows who lives at the next gate. A rural societal breakdown in which you have to go to nearby towns and cities for most community services, recreation, schools, churches, civic clubs. Very, very few rural merchants left. Far fewer farmers. And Reuben, there are so many poor on welfare, the obesity, the poor diets, really…and health care is not delivering equal services to rural folk. There are just not enough supportive personnel: physiotherapists, nurses and others who could teach health care and nutrition. We could be so much more preventative and proactive in health and education…save people so much anguish, and the taxpayer lots of money."

"This seems to be the way of the world now, Laura. We all have sweaty hands when we think of what might happen next. All of this you're talking about is compounded by ugly politics, global trade issues, uncertainty in the workplace, religious conflicts, dangerous leadership such as Putin. And Trump! The most worrisome candidate for President we've ever seen, building walls between nations, vicious flat-out ugly remarks. Did you catch him Wednesday night?"

"Yes, I heard it all. He's the first climate-denying potential head-of state in the world, too. Global warming, a Chinese hoax? He'd bomb countries to get their oil. He'd treat scientists and environmentalists as threats to the state. He was so angry, snarling, aggrieved and terrifying on Wednesday night… It's now five o'clock. I must prepare supper for us, Reuben."

But Reuben had brought prepared food from Belleville and had gone out to the car. When she told him to bring in his luggage, he nodded his head. His gaze turned soft and sad, she thought.

He had brought salads, warm spinach ravioli with rosé sauce, focaccia bread, wine, an apricot slice. "What a feast, Reuben."

Laura led him up the stairs with his luggage in hand and into the guest room. She carried with her a large pitcher of water and poured it into a large china basin. "A step back in time, Reuben." She showed him the bathroom opposite the guest room on their way back downstairs.

As she set the table in the large front room with the big, low windows, Reuben noticed the portraits that still hung on the wall near the old cranked telephone. "There are Ebenezer and Ann Dedham staring at us with approval, Laura."

The food and wine proved to be delicious. Reuben had been able to get those sticky old windows raised. She opened the front door, thankful she'd added a screen door last year when Anderson had put on the new roof.

As they dined, Reuben spoke of his early life in Belleville and mentioned the synagogue, now down to twenty-five families and hard-pressed to make enough to keep the building in repair. Laura made a mental note to send a small donation from her father's fund.

She introduced him to a new and favourite website she had discovered, *Common Dreams*, and introduced the subject of the Anthropocene Epoch. "I guess you could call it an era where human beings have become a geological force, Reuben. We are now more numerous than any mammal or plant on the earth. In the early eighteen-hundreds, the total world population was one billion people. In the last two hundred years, we've grown to seven billion, can you imagine? We have violated the species of the planet. We outnumber rats and even mice, and each of us is bigger than any one of them. DDT, hormones and plastics, everywhere those damned plastics. It's time to declare the eleven thousand-seven-hundred-year Holocene Epoch over."

Reuben removed a notebook and pen from his shirt pocket. Still the physician, he jotted down the website. "I think this has something, or is it everything to do with erosion rates, large-scale chemical perturbations to cycles of elements… long-lasting changes, some irreversible."

"Yes, Reuben, and the article lists them: climate change, plastics, fertilizers. This article refers one to other sites. I prefer going to the library, but I sure appreciate Google."

After supper, Reuben helped her with the dishes. How nice. After the cleanup they walked the yard and the barn lane, but it was still muggy and hot. Dusk was falling over the valley.

"No frogs, Reuben, I haven't heard any frogs."

"I'd like to go down to the river tomorrow," he replied. "Is that old lane still open? The one from Lloyd's farm into the swimming hole?"

"Your memory is phenomenal, Reuben."

"Well, Laura, it was just down the road from the store, and so much fun going there with you. How could I forget?"

Back on the porch, they sat until dark.

"Reuben, I have to tell you that I dreamed of you earlier this morning. I dreamed that Mother was beside me, sleeping. Strange, and I woke her up and cried, *Mother, I have to call the hospital. I have to talk to Reuben. I have to hear that he's alive…* I wept, Reuben. Now you're here."

"I'm awfully sorry, Laura."

"No, Reuben, don't feel sorry. I mention the dream because here you are sitting beside me tonight…"

"I didn't forget you. I came back. I hope I haven't upset you."

"No, Reuben. I am so happy. You must never think that I am unhappy."

"I left. I shouldn't have."

"It is only stupid to review decisions. You know that, you do know that. It's sappy, really," she snapped.

"You never married. Why?"

"I did not meet anyone. No other man who I could ever live with. Never anyone as handsome, as intelligent or as witty as you, of course." She laughed, but her brittle laughter shocked her. "I'm too cranky, Reuben."

"At our age we are entitled to be cranky," he replied. His laughter sounded soft, as it always had.

She asked him if he would like to go to Ormsby tomorrow. "A tearoom, very pleasant, and we can take the old Hastings road. I have yet to find that Hole-in-the-Wall Hill."

7

Laura hoped that the trip to Ormsby would not exhaust them beyond endurance. The heat wave, according to the weather service of the Canadian Broadcasting Corporation, had been forecasting cooler temperatures for the past three days. *Oops, wrong again, boys!* It would be hot and humid by midday, and the total time to drive and eat would be, comfortably, three to four hours. Reuben preferred to keep to the plan and perhaps stop at Walliston Lake for a swim, but Laura vetoed him. Another day.

Shortly after daybreak, they set out to walk the farm lane to the river. Heavy dew had forced them into knee-high rubber boots.

"Are you sure about this, Reuben? We could turn back now."

But Reuben smiled and moved steadily forward, glancing at Laura, who frowned. "I guess we could try. Reuben, look at that old post-and-rail. When Ebenezer came here in 1830, he cut the cedars to make the fences along this laneway, and it's still serving well. Around here they call this a snake fence. Ebenezer also planted these maples as saplings. And what a wonderful windbreak they form, and they sure protect the topsoil from blowing away. All along my fence lines."

"What did you find out about his background?"

"Sadly, my initial enquiries revealed very little. The birth and marriage records had been lost in a fire at the Records

Office in Essex, a short distance north-east of London. Local church records show Ebenezer's birth but nothing for his wife, Ann Whittaker. Military records show that he enlisted with the 66th Foot Regiment on the Isle of Wight, far away from Essex. Many mysteries, difficult to piece together. His years in service lasted from 1814 to 1817, being discharged with infection of the eye and admitted to the Royal Chelsea Pensioners Hospital in London. Then I find out that his name appears on a marriage certificate to Ann Whittaker in 1819 in Cheapside. The witnesses had signed with an X, probably picked them up from the street.

"Because Ebenezer wanted to emigrate to Canada, the law required that he be an Anglican in order to be eligible for a Crown Grant of land. He probably had been a Chapel man or a Methodist or some other unacceptable faith. Incidentally, Reuben, do you know that Quakers and Jews were exempted from this requirement? But Reuben, what a joke, I found birth records for his three children, proving that they had been baptized in a Chapel Church."

They were standing now in the tall grass, still wet with the early morning dew, and she guessed they might not make it to the river.

"Shall we continue, Reuben?"

"Of course," he replied, offering his arm. "Fascinating family, a history that deserves to be filed in Public Archives despite the unanswerable questions. Besides, I like being beside you in the dew." His eyes laughed.

Glancing at Reuben, Laura went on. "After Ebenezer arrived in Upper Canada, he was promised land along the Trent River in Cramahe Township. But for some reason, that land did not end up in his hands. No explanation. I know he had lived there in the late 1820s because his signature is on a petition to keep the town property agricultural to limit expansion. At that time of my research, I had found the Crown Patent for this property. That's all I have. Couldn't get any further, and frankly I lost interest."

They had to make a choice now: Continue to the river or return to the house, breakfast, and head north. It was 9:30 a.m. Soaked, they returned to the house.

"I'm bushed, Laura." Reuben appeared pale. Laura insisted that he get into some dry clothing.

"I'll hang these duds out to dry," he replied.

"I'll hang them out. Put them over the bannister."

Laura began to prepare a late breakfast. She set the coffee to brew. Reuben suggested that he make an omelette. She insisted they stay home, sleep, read, relax. It was too darned hot to go anywhere. Reuben said they might jump under the sprinkler. Laura vetoed that. The well at the house has only three feet of water, she told him, but the water in the barn well was clean, cool and plentiful. They would both struggle up there to jump and play, she said to him. She giggled.

After breakfast…what do you think, dear reader? They fell asleep and slept until three in the afternoon. And you know as well as I do, they slept in that double bed in the downstairs room.

8

Later that same day, still beastly hot, Laura and Reuben were rooting around in the bone-dry garden for any edible vegetable whatsoever which could be cooked and consumed alongside the steak they would barbeque. Pickings were slim for no rain had fallen since the end of June, just one searing day after the other.

"This pigweed certainly thrives," said Laura, bending over the row to pull out the noxious weed. She looked up at Reuben and tossed her head back—a gesture he had come to hold dear. A car on the highway revved up the steep grade on its way south to Madoc. He heard her give out a harsh laugh as she muttered something about *the bad weeds around the territory. To my mind, it's entertainment to run their hot rods up and down this road.*

Reuben bent to spade the rock-hard soil, pulled a few straggled carrots and threw them into the basket. He felt so beaten by this constant heat, and knew that Laura was at the end of her tether with nagging worries about reaping a harvest on land without rainfall.

He found himself thinking that if the drought continued over several years, permanent damage to the soil might force Laura to abandon the land. Who was around to call upon for help? What did this mean for himself? He thought of the current news journals he had brought with him.

One article had warned of a new strain of virus on the rise. Worldwide!

Reuben, on his hands and knees in the dirt, pushed himself to his feet. He dug his heels in, but they were not able to penetrate the flat, hard soil. A bit dizzy, he wiped his palms on his pants. "Do you have *anyone* around who could lend a hand with the work, Laura?"

"They'd find me, I gather." He saw that she looked away grimly.

"But are you not worried, somewhat, living alone here?"

"My niece checks in. Once every so often." Laura scanned her once green valley sloping down to the Moira River and ran her gaze northward. "See that line of trees on the horizon? That's the end of the fertile land in these parts. Up and over there," she pointed northward. "Up this Hastings Road, Reuben, away off and into the bush. The countryside is full of strangers now. Everything is different."

He didn't respond. He understood her concerns. She didn't have to say much more, out here in the dust and heat. He saw the truth of her condition.

Sadness came. Like a muted bell, her voice tolled, "As old-time farm families died out, their children didn't want farming any more. Too much hard labour, a farm. Enticed by cities. They got this from the movies, Reuben. Oh, there were some who stayed and *made a go of it*, even developing large tracts of farmland. But most of the fellows were starstruck and chose the bright lights. Presently, the folk with little education make do with minimum wage jobs in a factory. Or, just go on welfare. The more resourceful find work to pay for college courses, some train as nurses, doctors, or teachers. Many simply leave to work in Hogtown, and the ones who stay have a long drive to work, a long, long way to go to make a living wage. At day's end, they come home tired and disgruntled. The roads are so hazardous. They dart, Reuben. They speed. Cars make noise. Cars pollute. It's become so dangerous, what with more rain and ice on the roads in these warming winters.

"It's not good, not sound. Take note, Reuben. Widened, raised highways are so close to dwellings that the windows rattle. They have to deal with that noise and pollution. No time for socializing anymore. Very few visits with neighbours. Community dinners few and far between. Nobody has time, they say. Lived here all my life, Reuben, and hardly anyone knows my name."

"Tell me, how often does she visit, this niece?"

"Not often." Laura murmured. She looks directly at him and said, "We should get back and clean up, Reuben. Enough scrounging a few measly vegetables." She turned away. "This winter we might be pressed into begging. Sorry. Foolish gibberish."

* * *

At the kitchen sink, it took Reuben some time to scrub long, skinny, wobbly carrots before turning his hands to the few potatoes. The small bunch of kale, he figured, would taste mighty bitter in late August. He chopped the onions, tasted the parsley. Quite tough but, after all, what's a body to expect of vegetables with no rain? He stood back and admired the basket of food. Not so bad. Shiny clean. He shook his head in wonderment. He was speaking aloud in old-time Hastings County patter.

They decided to wait until dusk to barbeque, but this proved wrong. Millions of tiny flies, which Laura could not for the world identify, buzzed circles around them.

"It's a sign of plague, Reuben. That old Pharaoh, King Greed, has descended on us. I'm worried about this drought.

How long will this continue? What other disaster will come our way? Am I driving you crazy?"

"Not at all. You are a thoughtful person who stays alert to the situation, and that is the primary rule I learned in medical school. I am very, very concerned about the probability of another plague that could attack our global village."

"It seems a lifetime since Marshall McLuhan coined that phrase, Reuben."

"'How Long Has This Been Going On.' Remember that song?"

"I never was a pop follower, so I really don't know. The song was a big hit at the time, I guess. It had appeal, I believe, to all those errant people of the Sixties who committed adultery."

The dinner was delicious, and he promised to vacuum the flies away in the morning. It was sure hell when they turned the lights on to wash the dishes, but they managed to wash and dry and put them away fast.

"Whoever wants to get up in the morning to dirty dishes?" she murmured. They didn't say any more. She switched off the lights, turned on the flashlight. He opened the door to the downstairs bedroom. They removed their clothing, switched off the flashlight, rolled onto the bed and lay there sweating.

"How much longer will this heat wave last, do you think, Reuben?"

"Don't worry. The breeze should come in soon. Have I opened the windows?"

"I checked before. They are open."

"Do you think, Laura, this could become a habit with us?"

"Possibly, Reuben. I'm so happy, but I always preferred the word *possibly*. I like the sound of *poss-i-bly*."

"Okay, so we should talk it over, Laura."

"Okay." She sounded very drowsy.

"Goodnight."

During the night, Reuben awoke and could not fall back asleep. The dance had been held so many years ago, fifty-nine surely. He remembered the Orange Hall north of Eldorado. They had hardly spoken as they danced every dance. The following morning, Mr. Burns had approached him just as he was getting into his car to leave for Maynooth with the goods his father had given him to sell.

Reuben remembered standing before Mr. Burns. "How are you this morning, Mr. Burns?" he had asked.

"Fine, Reuben, but I am concerned. Laura is very young. Please, I want you to understand. She is far too young and you are seven years older. You have years of work to become a Doctor of Medicine, and it's going to take all of your time and attention. Speak with me, son, on your way back. Stop in. Please."

Reuben felt shaken. Truly, Laura was seven years younger than himself. Mr. Burns would be adamant, just as his parents would undoubtedly give him a clear message of disapproval, more probably a total rejection.

Reuben had telephoned Laura from Maynooth and arranged to meet her in Tweed. They sat in his car facing the beach at Stoco Lake. He told her that he had to quit seeing her. He had to return for his third year Med at Queens in Kingston. The toughest year. "Just too far away," he had said. He sweated. She sat there and didn't move. He told her that he faced a tough curriculum and would have to put in hours of study. He apologized, feeling foolish. He wanted to say that he loved her, that he was a bastard for betraying her, but he didn't. What was left for him were her last words.

You'll come back for me, Reuben. We'll have the life we talked about, your children, and later, I can be a part-time teacher. We have the same ideas about religion and politics, society, education. We were born for each other. I'll wait for you.

He nodded, he agreed. He placated her "I'll see, I don't really know yet."

She wept. He said he would call, he would write. But he never did call. He never did write.

* * *

In the middle of the night, he muttered, "Life stinks, Laura, and it's over too soon."

"Never blaspheme, Reuben." Laura was awake.

"It would have been so easy."

"Stop," she whispered. "I want to go with you to see your son, Jonathan."

"Okay, Laura, okay. Go back to sleep, *pitzele*. Sleep, sleep, sleep."

9

Morning fog, diffusing through a tangerine sunrise, greeted Laura and Reuben, both wide awake at six o'clock Friday morning. He heard Laura murmur something about the side door being left open all night because a swampy, sewage-like smell was coming up from the lowlands near the river.

Reuben stepped off the porch and walked out onto the grass. He wondered if the smell might possibly be still oozing from that old outside privy attached to the side of the driveshed.

"I've lived here since 1980, Reuben, and never before has that marshy smell been as strong as this. I'll go put the coffee on." She had never been through such heat either, she thought.

Reuben felt concerned about the tragic tone of her speech, her obvious effort to maintain herself from breaking down totally. But the heat of the sun was so intense even at this early hour, he could feel his skin burning through the shirt on his back. He checked his wristwatch: seven-thirty a.m. He walked onto the back porch.

The coffee had been made in an old percolator. "My mother always perked her coffee. She thought it gave the best flavor. Thank you, Laura."

In the surrounding silence, he heard the mantle clock tick through the open kitchen window, a faint hum from the refrigerator. A couple of crows cawed from the hill behind the barn.

"When I think of it, Laura, we have a great deal in common. First, we both have roots in rural living. My great-grandfather, my grandfather, *and* my father lived in the hills of Bukovina, which was then a region of the Austro-Hungarian Empire, now part of Romania. My people were landowners with orchards, sheep and goats. They had a few fields on which they grew cereal crops. I remember my dad, in his old age, saying how much he loved eating the bulgar. He could never forget the plum jam, repeatedly talking about boiling the plums in a huge iron cauldron over an open fire. He described how he and his brothers—fastened to a yoke— had had to walk round and round in a circle for up to nine hours, stirring the jam as it thickened, then ladling it into jars, and off to market. Dad talked about the horse that kept stopping and farting all the way to the village. And Dad's eyes would twinkle at Mom, across the table, glaring at him."

"They must have hooked paddles onto the yoke, Reuben, and there must have been some way to lower them into the cauldron."

Laura understood mechanical devices. Reuben noticed that her eyes sparkled with good health, with life

"I never made that trip back to Romania. I wanted to, but never did. Would you be interested in visiting that part of the world?"

"A carefully planned tour, Reuben, would be the best. It should be possible to arrange a tour through a Jewish tour agency in Toronto."

"The writer Aharon Appelfeld came from Bukovina. He has written numerous novels and other books about Jewish life in that region, including the extermination of the Jews under the Nazis and the flight of survivors to Israel. He is regarded as one of the Israel's finest."

"I'm sure I can get these books, Reuben, through interlibrary loan."

"I'll phone Jack Schecter, our librarian at the Greenberg Families Library in Ottawa. He's a wonderfully helpful person whom I greatly admire. He'll send them through to your library, or I could buy all of Applefeld's books for you."

He saw a warm, loving expression in her eyes this time when she asked, "Tell me about how you arrived in Canada with your family. I realize that you told me, but it's been so many years."

"We came over in June of 1935 when I was only two and a half years old. My dad had heard bad news. The Nazi Party was to meet in Nuremburg to consider a set of laws which would strip all German Jews of their citizenship and prevent inter-marriage with Christians. In Bukovina, the National Christian Party had already introduced discriminatory laws. Violence against Jews had become a daily occurrence.

"My dad was a man of action. He left with Mother and me. No horsing around. He got out, but I remember . . . he would say, *If Hitler had only been a madman, a meshugener, a con man, a gonif, I could understand, but Adolph Hitler was a Jew-hater like none other*. Genocide became a first priority of the Third Reich." They sat at the kitchen table now. Reuben reached for his glass of water.

"Before he died, Dad told me that my mother had been an awful problem to him before emigration, threatening to keep me with her and refusing to go with him. She relented, but I don't ever think—even when the count came in at six million souls—that she ever forgave him. She had come from a wealthy, sophisticated and assimilated family. And boy, she rammed that into us—me and Dad—for years. To be frank, my mother was a bigot. But she…she was the legs for my father at business. I guess they got along, as the saying goes.

"Dad chose the town of Belleville and the place served him well. We were accepted, even honoured and respected by local businessmen and professionals. Never had a bad look or an incident throughout the years that I am aware of.

"Dad had chosen Belleville for its size, and for its position halfway between Toronto and Montreal, with excellent rail transportation, a small well-established and dedicated Jewish community that went as far back as the eighteen thirties with the establishment of the *Belleville Intelligencer* by one George Benjamin, a Jew. Later came the Frank family, the Cominskys, the Tobes and others. We were involved with the Trenton air force base, especially after Dad sold the wholesale division of his clothing and dry goods business and established himself as the preferred manufacturer of military uniforms. He kept on with the production of civilian coats and suits. He became well-off."

Laura poured orange juice into his glass. "I know your grandparents died naturally, Reuben, but what happened to your other folks over there?"

"Wiped out. Mother suffered from depression after the war as word kept trickling in from Europe. She travelled back to her hometown to see if there were any survivors. Her mother and three brothers and most Bukovina Jews had been deported to concentration camps in Transnistria in 1942, which turned out to be a killing field, death by shootings, starvation, exposure and disease. She discovered that a few cousins had made it to Israel. She was never the same after that visit. She died in 1974. I can't go on anymore, Laura. I don't want to talk anymore. *May their memory be as a blessing…*"

"I understand so well, Reuben. My father was at Juno Beach."

They removed the dishes from the kitchen table. She kept rubbing the oilcloth table cover over and over for several minutes. He took her hands into his. "I want you to talk to me about this, your father at Juno Beach."

Laura washed the dishes with a small amount of hot water and soap and followed by rinsing them in a small amount of vinegar and water. He dried, polishing each dish and utensil slowly, carefully, and set them aside on the counter. Laura poured all the water she had used into a pail. She saved waste water for the plants, the vegetable garden.

"What a lot of work," she sighed, looking out the north window that was set above the sink. "I keep my eyes fixed on the horizon, Reuben. The line of conifers there and the highway running northward through them. I concentrate on the horizon this summer.

"At Juno, Dad is the first off the landing craft because he leads his section of the platoon. Bullets—whatever the hell— hit the water, cut down the men in front of him. He runs down the ramp, hunched over, making it to the beach. He didn't stop to look back until he reached the protection of the seawall. As each man had been instructed to do. No one was to stop or look back. At the seawall, he turned to find his men. Not one of his twelve men had made it. He couldn't go back for them. He just stepped in beside the others who were climbing the seawall to get into the town.

"My father may be the reason why I never married. The war broke him. He came back a different man, my mother had told me, when once we'd found him slumped in a chair with an empty bottle on the floor beside him. He'd been watching a film of the Juno Beach landing, again. Damned right, he came back a different man, Reuben."

She sat down abruptly, held her head in her hands. Her face contorted, turned red. "He lost his men at Juno Beach and blamed himself because he followed bloody orders like they all did, Reuben. Follow bloody orders and kill each other. Millions and millions, but don't add it for me. I don't want to hear the numbers anymore. I've stopped counting the numbers murdered in the last century. For what? Look around. The young are lost—not all—but so many homeless, without purpose, unable to concentrate, obese, sick, deformed, drugged. I saw a boy in Belleville the other day, staggering. He placed one foot over the other, striving to walk, catching himself on a post, the side of a building, trying to balance himself. I followed him, Reuben. 'Son,' I says, 'what's wrong with you?' But he wouldn't or couldn't even get the words out. I called 911, Reuben, and they gave me hell for trying to help him. What is happening in our country?"

Reuben took her in his arms and suggested a swim in the Quinte Centre pool. He telephoned. They were open. Laura nodded. He drove her to Belleville to swim in cool, clear, salted and chlorinated water.

10

"Which road should I take home, Laura?"

"Whose home do you mean?" She laughed. "That depends on whose home you want to live in. Do you want me…or not?" He did not laugh.

He pulled away from the Centre and, taking a right turn onto Highway 37, proceeded north toward Tweed. "It's very scenic, a better road than 62."

As they drove through the outskirts of Belleville, she spoke quietly: "Perhaps we should keep both homes as options. It would be sensible, for a limited time. It is very complicated trying to live in two places. I've heard horror stories from a friend who says that it drives her mad never knowing where anything is, and washing and shopping for two houses, not to mention the cleaning, Reuben, and that farm requires someone to tend it every day."

"Remember, Laura, I spent my first years here until I went to Montreal for my internship in 1959. I'm twenty-six years old by then. I considered us engaged during all those years at University and Med School in Kingston. I spent every spare day and night at your house almost, except for being home with my parents."

He stopped speaking, realizing that his mistake had been to go to Montreal for his internship year. He should never have gone that far away.

"A clincher year, Montreal, Laura," he sighed. "Separation kills relationships. That's what happened. I followed the trend of the day, thinking that I could keep our relationship, even from far away. Remember when people started to say, *I spend little time with my wife and kids, but when I do, it's quality time?*"

"Reuben, this is another reason why I never married. I decided that I'd rather be alone than lonely. I did have lots to do, what with teaching and my curiosity about everything… Let's stop in Tweed for lunch. There's a nice café there."

Sitting at a quiet table, Reuben murmured, "In the fragment of time the Holy One allots, should a person choose to live alone?"

"Where would we live, Reuben?" she said, nibbling at the greens on her plate.

"The farm, of course. I'd be coming back to my roots. I could fix up the place, if you wish. I'm sure we could belong to Sons of Jacob, and they need new members. I can give you a book, *Introduction to Judaism*, that my rabbi gave me to read—and I'm supposed to be Jewish, but I still learned a lot from that book.

"I'd like that, and I'd be pleased to go with you to the synagogue, Reuben. Would you be able to help me drill a new well to replace the old dug well? Boy, oh boy that would be my dream come true, with you." Laura began to sing these words, and a few people looked around and stared at them.

Reuben loves her humour, her calm tenacity, possibly her stubbornness, but her beautiful chiseled jaw, her pageboy hair and poised demeanor are irresistible.

"As we are getting older, let's live it," he said. "I bet you would like my son. Jonathan lives in Old Hollywood with his wife, Ellen, and their three children, Adam, Sarah and Ezra. I am going to visit him in October for the High Holy Days, and you can come with me. Jonathan has a driver from the studio who will take us anywhere. Pacific Coast Highway, Malibu, Hearst Castle, the San Diego Zoo. Adam, my eldest grandson, nineteen years of age, is entering the rabbinate at the Hebrew Union College in L.A. How about that?"

"And you say that Jonathan's an agnostic? See what kids do to their parents, Reuben. Sorry to say, all I can do is laugh."

"Jonathan phoned me the other night. He said that he wants me near, and to come often. He wants to give me his love, he says, before it's too late. Laura, I'm not leaving this world so fast, my love."

They began to scheme a ridiculous list of choices for their new life together. Winters in L.A. with Jonathan, an extended road trip up the Gaspé and boat into St. Pierre et Miquelon, a desert hike along the National Israel Path, cruise the globe for maybe a year and boy, would that break the bank! Grow organic chickens, renovate the house and add that indoor pool, join the Stirling Theatre Guild, The Belleville Club and The Hastings County Historical Society, bird watch.

Laura loved Reuben's humour, his confidence, his strong physique, his presence, his breath, his skin and every cell in his body, his educated mind, his worldliness . . . and his faith.

That night, Laura dreams of her father, George Burns. He lies dead in the hospital. She stands over him. *Dad, wake up. I have to take measurements of you, your head, your arm, your old varicosed legs. I have to measure each part, your waist, thigh, the length of your hand, your foot to be sure, Dad.* Laura sees his profile, a remarkable, true English head, his jaw defined against the stark white hospital wall—the marbleized effigy of a monarch. Mother weeps by her side. Laura tries to move but she cannot. Her legs have seized . . .

"Wake up, Laura. You're having a nightmare. I'm here. It's only a dream." He switched on the bedside lamp.

"My father, Reuben, that dear old thing, my old dad."

He took her in his arms and held her. "Laura, remember the Gonsalus homestead and lake behind the place. We walked over there to see if it may be swimmable and it looked great. Let's try that again. That was a good pool of water and it spouted, remember. It was salty."

Together they spoke about that spring of water and hoped that all the springs would spout again. Reuben whispered the prayer for rain and he cries, whispering a few words about Jonathan that she couldn't hear clearly. They spoke of their common roots, of his grandfather's village Suceava, and of her ancestor Ebenezer Dedham, blinded by that *mamzer* Napoleon. She whispered that she loved him.

"Reuben, we might be a couple of articles for getting together at this stage of our lives, but don't for heaven's sake ever let us sell up and go to a retirement home."

EPILOGUE

75

Dear Reader,

Have you wondered why Israel and Jerusalem are mentioned thirteen times in this novella, including the Yehudah Amichai poem excerpt in the prologue?

I take you back to the Spring of 2018. Every day in the six weeks that Anne spent researching for *EREV,* we awoke in our suite at *Mishkenot Sha'ananim* Guest House in Jerusalem, drew open the curtains, stepped onto the long balcony, sat down with our cups of coffee, transfixed by the view across the Hinnom Valley at the Old City walls, the glow of the Golden Dome on Temple Mount in the background with its Western Wall so sacred to our people.

Floating panoramic visions of five thousand years of history holy to the three Abrahamic religions. The prophetic words of Yehudah Amichai that proclaims the eternal spiritual foundation of the nation Israel.

Inspiration for any creative person . . . tickling all the grey cells.

On a personal note, gratitude for the kindnesses of Mishkenot managers Rita and Orit, Sam at the front desk, and Meir Sayfan who went out of his way to help us, Montefiore Restaurant waiters Jubran and Rifke; Dan Shavit of Dani's Taxi. Over the six weeks we were there Dani squired us on visits to Latrun, the Palmach Museum in Tel Aviv, the Armoured Corps Museum in Latrun where we watched the induction of recruits receiving their bible and rifle, spurring memories of his IDF days, the Police Museum in Beit Shemesh, the Valley of Elah where David killed Goliath, Dani's favourite restaurants in Jaffa and Abu Gosh (home of "the best falafel and hummus in all the world"), and his stories as we travelled the forested small roads in the Judean Hills past vinyards and olive groves on the way from Latrun up to Jerusalem.

When we came down to earth and returned to Ottawa, Anne spent months completing a second draft of *EREV*. Anne told me that she now wanted to write a Part 2 in which Reuben and Laura would make pilgrimage to Jerusalem, but in order to lend credence to her writing she would once again need to be enveloped by City, Country, Hills, People.

Well, had it not been for the interference of COVID-19, there would have been a Part 2 rather than this monologue. Anne repeatedly expressed the feeling Laura and Reuben's companionship in the twilight of their lives would be enhanced and purposed by such a metaphorical journey.

Yeru and *shalayim,* 'flowing it's way to the completeness of peace.' Biblical peace: the wholeness of memories, inspiring resilience, offering hope. A message to all of us.

That's why Israel and Jerusalem are mentioned so often in the book.

Sol M. Shmelzer
June 20, 2021

GLOSSARY

Chapel Church (p. 57): chapels created by non-Anglicans during the 16th century Reformation

D'varim (p.38): Deuteronomy, fifth Book of the Jewish Torah

erev (book title): evening

fleishik, milchig, pareve (p. 18): foods with meat or milk or foods that are neutral, as set by Jewish dietary laws

gonif (p. 67): thief

halacha (p. 11): Jewish religious laws

Hogtown (p. 60): nickname for City of Toronto

kaddish (p. 33): prayer for the dead

kashrut (p. 18): Jewish dietary laws

kvetch (p. 19): to complain, complainer

kishkes (p. 41): Yiddish slang for guts, or intestines

la Sûreté (p. 26): police

Maariv (p. 27): evening prayer service

mamzer (p. 74): bastard

mein sohn (p. 14): my son

meshuga (p. 14): crazy

mishegaz (p. 23): crazy, idiosyncratic

Mishkenot Sha'ananim (p. 12): "Peaceful dwellings." Arts and culture centre with residence program for scholars, artists and writers

modeh ani (p. 18): I thank

pitzele (p. 64): dear little one

schlemiel (p. 31): a jerk, inept person

Shabbos (p. 11): Jewish sabbath, day of rest

shah (p. 25): quiet!

Shacharit (p. 11): morning prayer

Sheol (p. 33): afterlife

shiva (p. 14): seven days of mourning after a death

schmooze (p. 20): to chat

s'lichah (p. 11): excuse me

shul (p. 11): synagogue

Tanach (p. 38): The Jewish Scriptures, comprising the Torah (Books of Law), Prophets and collected Writings

tefillin (p. 18): phyllactories worn by Orthodox Jewish men in weekday morning prayers

tragerkeit umet (p. 28): sadness

yente (p. 19): Jewish gossip

yiddisher (p. 28): person who speaks Yiddish language

I wish to thank my husband, Sol Morton Shmelzer, for his authorial advice and constant encouragement, publishing consultant Allen Zuk, and literary editor, Jeff Karon, PhD, for bringing this book to publication and for their belief in this story.

This book stands as a tribute to the many persons who have given generously of their time in points of research, and those who have read and offered critiques. It has been my privilege to receive your expertise and support.

Anne Shmelzer is pleased to release a second work of fiction, *EREV: The Evening Years of Reuben Gurewitz*. Her award-winning memoir, *The Night My Father Came Back from the War* which appeared in the Ottawa Citizen served as a precursor to her debut novel, *A Marginally Noted Man*. Anne's extensive knowledge and experience as a psychiatric nurse helps shape her characters, and her years as a poet and accomplishments in music underscore the lyrical quality of her writing. She has also written musical and academic papers deposited in the National Library of Canada and the Henri de la Grange Library in Paris.

Born in 1940, Anne Shmelzer spent her childhood between Toronto and Madoc Township, Ontario. She attended the prestigious Lisgar Collegiate Institute where her love of writing was first nurtured. She went on to receive her Registered Nursing Diploma with a focus on psychiatry and later completed her Bachelor of Music High Honours from Carleton University. Anne has long been connected with those who seek to observe and notate the workings of the human heart. Anne lives in Ottawa with her husband, Sol Shmelzer.

Author Photograph by Mitch Lenet

NOTES

NOTES

NOTES